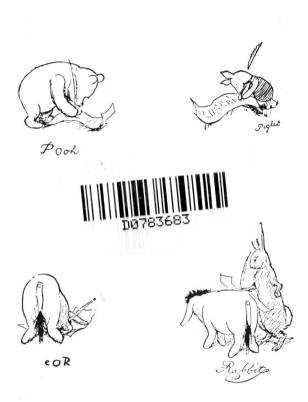

Pooh

Piglet

eOR

Rabbit

# Pooh's Alphabet Book

Methuen Children's Books · London

# POOH's
# Alphabet Book

❀ by A. A. MILNE ❀

illustrations by E. H. Shepard

Compilation copyright © 1975 by Sir Henry Chisholm,
John Frederick Lehmann, John Christopher Medley and
Michael John Brown, Trustees of the Pooh Properties

Text by A. A. Milne and illustrations by E. H. Shepard
from *Winnie the Pooh* and *The House at Pooh Corner*
copyright under the Berne Convention

Quotations selected by Ann Troy
Designed by Riki Levinson

Printed in Great Britain
by Hazell Watson & Viney Ltd
Aylesbury, Bucks

ISBN 0 416 49310 6

3 Cheers for Pooh!
(*For who?*)
For Pooh—

A

### Animal

"It is hard to be brave," said Piglet, sniffing slightly, "when you're only a Very Small Animal."

### Bear

"I am a Bear of Very Little Brain,
and long words Bother me."

B

Bear began to sigh, and then
found he couldn't because he was so
tightly stuck; and a tear rolled down
his eye, as he said:

"Then would you read a Sustain-
ing Book, such as would help and
comfort a Wedged Bear in Great
Tightness?"

## Christopher Robin

"I've got two names," said
Christopher Robin carelessly.

C

## Company

"Aha! If I know anything about anything, that hole means Rabbit, and Rabbit means Company, and Company means Food and Listening-to Me-Humming and such like."

D

### Day

"Many happy returns of the day,"
said Piglet.

"Meaning me?"

"Of course, Eeyore."

"My birthday?"

"Yes."

"Me having a real birthday?"

"Yes, Eeyore, and I've brought you
a present."

### Eat

And then, suddenly, he remembered. He had eaten Eeyore's birthday present!

### Eeyore

"And how are you?" said Winnie-
the-Pooh.

Eeyore shook his head from side
to side.

"Not very how," he said. "I don't
seem to have felt at all how for a
long time."

### Forest

"You know how it is in the Forest. One can't have *anybody* coming into one's house. One has to be *careful*. What about a mouthful of something?"

### Friend

"Eeyore," he said solemnly, "I, Winnie-the-Pooh, will find your tail for you."

"Thank you, Pooh," answered Eeyore. "You're a real friend," said he. "Not like Some," he said.

### Grandfather

Pooh was wondering what a
Grandfather was like, and if perhaps
this was Two Grandfathers they
were after now, and, if so, whether
he would be allowed to take one
home and keep it.

G

### Heffalump

"Bother!" said Pooh. "It all comes
of trying to be kind to Heffalumps!"

## Honey

"I just like to know," said Pooh
humbly. "So as I can say to myself:
'I've got fourteen pots of honey left.'
Or fifteen, as the case may be. It's
sort of comforting."

### Idea

And then he had a Clever Idea. He would go up very quietly to the Six Pine Trees now, peep very cautiously into the Trap, and see if there *was* a Heffalump there. And if there was, he would go back to bed, and if there wasn't, he wouldn't.

I

There was a moment's silence
while everybody thought.

"I've got a sort of idea," said Pooh
at last, "but I don't suppose it's a very
good one."

"I don't suppose it is either," said
Eeyore.

### Jagular

The Jagular called out to them.
"Help! Help!" it called.

"That's what Jagulars always do,"
said Pooh, much interested. "They
call 'Help! Help!' and then when you
look up, they drop on you."

"I'm looking *down*," cried Piglet
loudly, so as the Jagular shouldn't
do the wrong thing by accident.

J

### Kanga

"Don't open the mouth, dear, or the soap goes in," said Kanga. "There! What did I tell you?"

"You—you—you did it on purpose," spluttered Piglet.

1. *General Remarks.* Kanga runs
faster than any of Us, even Me.

2. *More General Remarks.* Kanga
never takes her eye off Baby Roo,
except when he's safely buttoned up
in her pocket.

L

## Love

"Oh, Bear!" said Christopher
Robin, "How I do love you!"
"So do I," said Pooh.

### Mistake

Christopher Robin went back to lunch with his friends Pooh and Piglet, and on the way they told him of the Awful Mistake they had made. And when he had finished laughing, they all sang the Outdoor Song for Snowy Weather the rest of the way home.

M

N

### Noise

"What can it be?" Pooh thought.
"There are lots of noises in the
Forest, but this is a different one.
It isn't a growl, and it isn't a purr,
and it isn't a bark, and it isn't the
noise-you-make-before-beginning-a-
piece-of-poetry, but it's a noise of
some kind, made by a strange
animal. And he's making it outside
my door. So I shall get up and ask
him not to do it."

### Owl

"And if anyone knows anything about anything," said Bear to himself, "it's Owl who knows something about something," he said, "or my name's not Winnie-the-Pooh," he said. "Which it is," he added. "So there you are."

O

PLEZ CNOKE
IF AN RNSR
IS NOT REQID

### Pooh and Piglet

"Tigger is all right *really*," said Piglet lazily.

"Of course he is," said Christopher Robin.

"Everybody is *really*," said Pooh. "That's what *I* think," said Pooh. "But I don't suppose I'm right," he said.

"Of course you are," said Christopher Robin.

Piglet sidled up to Pooh from behind.

"Pooh!" he whispered.

"Yes, Piglet?"

"Nothing," said Piglet, taking Pooh's paw. "I just wanted to be sure of you."

### Queen Bee

"We must be practical. The important bee to deceive is the Queen Bee. Can you see which is the Queen Bee from down there?"

"No."

Q

### Rabbit

"Rabbit," said Pooh to himself, "I *like* talking to Rabbit. He talks about sensible things. He doesn't use long, difficult words, like Owl. He uses short, easy words, like 'What about lunch?' and 'Help yourself, Pooh.' I suppose *really*, I ought to go and see Rabbit."

R

### Roo

"Tigger *dear!*" said Kanga.

"He's taken my medicine, he's taken my medicine, he's taken my medicine!" sang Roo happily, thinking it was a tremendous joke.

### Spelling

For Owl, wise though he was in many ways, able to read and write and spell his own name WOL, yet somehow went all to pieces over delicate words like MEASLES and BUTTERED TOAST.

WOL

S

"My spelling is Wobbly. It's good
spelling but it Wobbles, and the
letters get in the wrong places."

T

### Tigger

"All I did was I coughed," said Tigger.

"He bounced," said Eeyore.

"Well, I sort of boffed," said Tigger.

"Hush!" said Rabbit, holding up his paw. "What does Christopher Robin think about it all? That's the point."

### Umbrella

"Have you an umbrella in your house?"

"I think so."

"I wish you would bring it out here, and walk up and down with it, and look up at me every now and then, and say 'Tut-tut, it looks like rain.' I think, if you did that, it would help the deception which we are practicing on these bees."

## Useful

"Well, it's a very nice pot, even if there's no honey in it, and if I washed it clean, and got somebody to write '*A Happy Birthday*' on it, Eeyore could keep things in it, which might be Useful."

V

### Verse

"This is the first verse," Pooh said
to Piglet.

"First verse of what?"

"My song."

"What song?"

"This one."

"Which one?"

"Well, if you listen, Piglet, you'll
hear it."

"How do you know I'm not
listening?"

### Winnie-the-Pooh

"He's Winnie-ther-Pooh. Don't you know what '*ther*' means?"

"Ah, yes, now I do," I said quickly; and I hope you do too, because it is all the explanation you are going to get.

X

### Expotition

"We are all going on an Expedition," said Christopher Robin.

"Going on an Expotition?" said Pooh eagerly, "I don't think I've ever been on one of those. Where are we going to on this Expotition?"

"Expedition, silly old Bear. It's "got an 'x' in it."

"Oh!" said Pooh. "I know." But he didn't really.

## Yesterday

"I think," said Piglet, when he had licked the tip of his nose too, and found that it brought very little comfort, "I think that I have just remembered something that I forgot to do *yesterday* and shan't be able to do tomorrow. So I suppose I really ought to go back and do it now."

Y

Z

### BuZZ

"That buzzing-noise means something. You don't get a buzzing-noise like that, just buzzing and buzzing, without its meaning something. If there's a buzzing-noise, somebody's making a buzzing-noise, and the only reason for making a buzzing-noise that *I* know of is because you're a bee."

Kanga

WOL